In the topmost story of the castle the Lady
Aurora occupied a spacious apartment of several
large rooms looking southward. The windows
projected oriel-wise over the garden below, and
there was a splendid view from them both up
and down and across the river. The opposite side
of the valley was steep, but not very high. Far
away snowpeaks were visible. These rooms
Aurora seldom left, but their airy spaces, the
brilliant landscape and sky, the plentiful sunlight, the musical instruments, books, pictures,
curiosities, with the company of Watho, who
made herself charming, precluded all dullness.
She had venison and feathered game to eat, milk
and pale sunny sparkling wine to drink.

She had hair of the yellow gold, waved and
rippled; her skin was fair, not white like
Watho's, and her eyes were of the blue of the
heavens when bluest; her features were delicate
but strong, her mouth large and finely curved,
and haunted with smiles.

BEHIND THE CASTLE THE HILL ROSE ABRUPTLY; the northeastern tower, indeed, was in contact with the rock and communicated with the interior of it. For in the rock was a series of chambers, known only to Watho and the one servant whom she trusted, called Falca. Some former owner had constructed these chambers after the tomb of an Egyptian king, and probably with the same design, for in the center of one of them stood what could only be a sarcophagus, but that and others were walled off. The sides and roofs of them were carved in low relief, and curiously painted. Here the witch lodged the blind lady, whose name was Vesper. Her eyes were black, with long black lashes; her skin had a look of darkened silver, but was of purest tint and grain; her hair was black and fine and straight flowing; her features were exquisitely formed, and if less beautiful yet more lovely from sadness; she always looked as if she wanted to lie down and not rise again. She did not know she was lodged in a tomb, though now and then she wondered she never touched a window. There were many couches, covered with richest silk, and soft as her own cheek, for her to lie upon; and the carpets were so thick, she might have cast herself down anywhere—as befitted a tomb. The place was dry and warm, and cunningly pierced for air, so that it was always fresh, and lacked only sunlight. There the witch fed her upon milk, and wine dark as a carbuncle, and pomegranates, and purple grapes, and birds that dwell in marshy places; and she played to her mournful tunes, and caused wailful violins to attend her, and told her sad tales, thus holding her ever in an atmosphere of sweet sorrow.

ATHO AT LENGTH HAD HER DESIRE, FOR witches often get what they want: a splendid boy was born to the fair Aurora. Just as the sun rose, he opened his eyes. Watho carried him immediately to a distant part of the castle, and persuaded the mother that he never cried but once, dying the moment he was born. Overcome with grief, Aurora left the castle as soon as she was able, and Watho never invited her again.

And now the witch's care was that the child should not know darkness. Persistently she trained him until at last he never slept during the day and never woke during the night. She never let him see anything black, and even kept all dull colors out of his way. Never, if she could help it, would she let a shadow fall upon him, watching against shadows as if they had been live things that would hurt him. All day he basked in the full splendor of the sun, in the same large rooms his mother had occupied. Watho used him to the sun, until he could bear more of it than any dark-blooded African. In the hottest of every day, she stripped him and laid him in it, that he might ripen like a peach; and the boy rejoiced in it, and would resist being dressed again. She brought all her knowledge to bear on making his muscles strong and elastic and swiftly responsive—that his soul, she said laughingly, might sit in every fiber, be all in every part, and awake the moment of call. His hair was of the red gold, but his eyes grew darker as he grew, until they were as black as Vesper's. He was the merriest of creatures, always laughing, always loving, for a moment raging, then laughing afresh. Watho called him Photogen.

IVE OR SIX MONTHS AFTER THE BIRTH OF
Photogen, the dark lady also gave birth to a
baby: in the windowless tomb of a blind mother,
in the dead of night, under the feeble rays of a
lamp in an alabaster globe, a girl came into the
darkness with a wail. And just as she was born
for the first time, Vesper was born for the
second, and passed into a world as unknown to
her as this was to her child—who would have
to be born yet again before she could see her
mother.

Watho called her Nycteris, and she grew as
like Vesper as possible—in all but one particu-
lar. She had the same dark skin, dark eyelashes
and brows, dark hair, and gentle sad look; but

she had just the eyes of Aurora, the mother of Photogen, and if they grew darker as she grew older, it was only a darker blue. Watho, with the help of Falca, took the greatest possible care of her—in every way consistent with her plans, that is—the main point in which was that she should never see any light but what came from the lamp. Hence her optic nerves, and indeed her whole apparatus for seeing, grew both larger and more sensitive; her eyes, indeed, stopped short only of being too large. Under her dark hair and forehead and eyebrows, they looked like two breaks in a cloudy night-sky, through which peeped the heaven where the stars and no clouds live. She was a sadly dainty little creature. No one in the world except those two was aware of the being of the little bat. Watho trained her to sleep during the day and wake during the night. She taught her music, in which she was herself a proficient, and taught her scarcely anything else.

THE HOLLOW IN WHICH THE CASTLE OF WATHO lay was a cleft in a plain rather than a valley among hills, for at the top of its steep sides, both north and south, was a tableland, large and wide. It was covered with rich grass and flowers, with here and there a wood, the outlying colony of a great forest. These grassy plains were the finest hunting grounds in the world. Great herds of small but fierce cattle, with humps and shaggy manes, roved about them, also antelopes and gnus, and the tiny roedeer, while the woods were swarming with wild creatures. The tables of the castle were mainly supplied from them. The chief of Watho's huntsmen was a fine fellow, and when Photogen began to outgrow the training she could give him, she handed him over to Fargu. He with a will set about teaching him all he knew. He got him pony after pony, larger and larger as he grew, every one less manageable than that which had preceded it, and advanced him from pony to horse, and from horse to horse, until he was equal to anything in that kind which the country produced. In similar fashion he trained him to the use of bow and arrow, substituting every three months a stronger bow and longer arrows; and soon he became, even on horseback, a wonderful archer. He was but fourteen when he killed his first bull, causing jubilation among the huntsmen, and indeed, through all the castle, for there too he was the favorite. Every day, almost as soon as the sun was up, he went out hunting, and would in general be out nearly the whole of the day. But Watho had laid upon Fargu just one commandment, namely, that Photogen should on no account, whatever the plea, be out until sundown, or so near it as to wake in him the desire of seeing what was going to happen; and this commandment Fargu was anxiously careful not to break; for although he

would not have trembled had a whole herd of
bulls come down upon him, charging at full
speed across the level, and not an arrow left in
his quiver, he was more than afraid of his mistress. When she looked at him in a certain way,
he felt, he said, as if his heart turned to ashes in
his breast, and what ran in his veins was no
longer blood, but milk and water. So that, ere
long, as Photogen grew older, Fargu began to
tremble, for he found it steadily growing harder
to restrain him. So full of life was he, as Fargu
said to his mistress, much to her content, that
he was more like a live thunderbolt than a hu-
man being. He did not know what fear was, and
that not because he did not know danger; for
he had had a severe laceration from the razor-
like tusk of a boar—whose spine, however, he
had severed with one blow of his hunting knife,
before Fargu could reach him with defense.
When he would spur his horse into the midst
of a herd of bulls, carrying only his bow and
his short sword, or shoot an arrow into a herd,
and go after it as if to reclaim it for a runaway
shaft, arriving in time to follow it with a spear

thrust before the wounded animal knew which way to charge, Fargu thought with terror how it would be when he came to know the temptation of the huddle-spot leopards, and the knife-clawed lynxes, with which the forest was haunted. For the boy had been so steeped in the sun, from childhood so saturated with his influence, that he looked upon every danger from a sovereign height of courage. When, therefore, he was approaching his sixteenth year, Fargu ventured to beg Watho that she would lay her commands upon the youth himself, and release him from responsibility for him. One might as soon hold a tawny-maned lion as Photogen, he said. Watho called the youth, and in the presence of Fargu laid her command upon him never to be out when the rim of the sun should touch the horizon, accompanying the prohibition with hints of consequences, none the less awful than they were obscure. Photogen listened respectfully, but, knowing neither the taste of fear nor the temptation of the night, her words were but sounds to him.

THE LITTLE EDUCATION SHE INTENDED NYCTERIS
to have, Watho gave her by word of mouth. Not
meaning she should have light enough to read
by, to leave other reasons unmentioned, she
never put a book in her hands. Nycteris, however, saw so much better than Watho imagined
that the light she gave her was quite sufficient,
and she managed to coax Falca into teaching her
the letters, after which she taught herself to
read, and Falca now and then brought her a
child's book. But her chief pleasure was in her
instrument. Her very fingers loved it and would
wander about its keys like feeding sheep. She
was not unhappy. She knew nothing of the
world except the tomb in which she dwelt, and

had some pleasure in everything she did. But she desired, nevertheless, something more or different. She did not know what it was, and the nearest she could come to expressing it to herself was—that she wanted more room. Watho and Falca would go from her beyond the shine of the lamp, and come again; therefore surely there must be more room somewhere. As often as she was left alone, she would fall to poring over the colored bas-reliefs on the walls. These were intended to represent various of the powers of Nature under allegorical similitudes, and as nothing can be made that does not belong to the general scheme, she could not fail at least to imagine a flicker of relationship between some of them, and thus a shadow of the reality of things found its way to her.

There was one thing, however, which moved and taught her more than all the rest—the lamp, namely, that hung from the ceiling, which she always saw alight, though she never saw the flame, only the slight condensation towards the center of the alabaster globe. And besides the operation of the light itself after its kind, the indefiniteness of the globe, and the softness of the light, giving her the feeling as if her eyes could go in and into its whiteness, were somehow also associated with the idea of space and room. She would sit for an hour together gazing up at the lamp, and her heart would swell as she gazed. She would wonder what had hurt her when she found her face wet with tears, and then would wonder how she could have been hurt without knowing it. She never looked thus at the lamp except when she was alone.

WATHO, HAVING GIVEN ORDERS, TOOK IT FOR granted they were obeyed, and that Falca was all night long with Nycteris, whose day it was. But Falca could not get into the habit of sleeping through the day, and would often leave her alone half the night. Then it seemed to Nycteris that the white lamp was watching over her. As it was never permitted to go out—while she was awake at least—Nycteris, except by shutting her eyes, knew less about darkness than she did about light. Also, the lamp being fixed high overhead, and in the center of everything, she did not know much about shadows either. The few there were fell almost entirely on the floor, or kept like mice about the foot of the walls.

Once, when she was thus alone, there came the noise of a far-off rumbling: she had never before heard a sound of which she did not know the origin, and here therefore was a new sign of something beyond these chambers. Then came a trembling, then a shaking; the lamp dropped from the ceiling to the floor with a great crash, and she felt as if both her eyes were hard shut and both her hands over them. She concluded that it was the darkness that had made the rumbling and the shaking, and rushing into the room, had thrown down the lamp. She sat trembling. The noise and the shaking ceased, but the light did not return. The darkness had eaten it up!

Her lamp gone, the desire at once awoke to get out of her prison. She scarcely knew what *out* meant; out of one room into another, where there was not even a dividing door, only an open arch, was all she knew of the world. But suddenly she remembered that she had heard Falca speak of the lamp *going out:* this must be what she had meant? And if the lamp had gone out, where had it gone? Surely where Falca went, and like her it would come again. But she could not wait. The desire to go out grew irresistible. She must follow her beautiful lamp! She must find it! She must see what it was about!

Now, there was a curtain covering a recess in the wall, where some of her toys and gymnastic things were kept; and from behind that curtain Watho and Falca always appeared, and behind it they vanished. How they came out of solid wall, she had not an idea, all up to the wall was open space, and all beyond it seemed wall; but clearly the first and only thing she could do was to feel her way behind the curtain. It was so dark that a cat could not have caught the largest of mice. Nycteris could see better than any cat, but now her great eyes were not of the smallest use to her. As she went she trod upon a piece of the broken lamp. She had never worn shoes or stockings, and the fragment, though, being of soft alabaster, it did not cut, yet hurt her foot. She did not know what it was, but as it had not been there before the darkness came, she suspected that it had to do with the lamp. She kneeled therefore, and searched with her hands, and bringing two large pieces together, recognized the shape of the lamp. Therefore it flashed upon her that the lamp was dead, that this brokenness was the death of which she had read without understanding, that the darkness had killed the lamp. What then could Falca have meant when she spoke of the lamp *going out*? There was the lamp—dead indeed, and so changed that she would never have taken it for a lamp but for the shape! No, it was not the lamp anymore now it was dead, for all that made it a lamp was gone, namely, the bright shining of it. Then it must be the shine, the light, that had gone out! That must be what Falca meant— and it must be somewhere in the other place in the wall. She started afresh after it, and groped her way to the curtain.

Now, she had never in her life tried to get out, and did not know how; but instinctively she began to move her hands about over one of the walls behind the curtain, half expecting them to go into it, as she supposed Watho and Falca did. But the wall repelled her with inexorable hardness, and she turned to the one opposite. In so doing, she set her foot upon an ivory die, and as it met sharply the same spot the broken alabaster had already hurt, she fell forward with her outstretched hands against the wall. Something gave way, and she tumbled out of the cavern.

BUT ALAS! OUT WAS VERY MUCH LIKE IN, FOR the same enemy, the darkness, was here also. The next moment, however, came a great gladness—a firefly, which had wandered in from the garden. She saw the tiny spark in the distance. With slow pulsing ebb and throb of light, it came pushing itself through the air, drawing nearer and nearer, with that motion which more resembles swimming than flying, and the light seemed the source of its own motion.

"My lamp! my lamp!" cried Nycteris. "It is the shiningness of my lamp, which the cruel darkness drove out. My good lamp has been waiting for me here all the time! It knew I would come after it, and waited to take me with it."

She followed the firefly, which, like herself, was seeking the way out. If it did not know the way, it was yet light; and, because all light is one, any light may serve to guide to more light. If she was mistaken in thinking it the spirit of her lamp, it was of the same spirit as her lamp—and had wings. The gold-green jet-boat, driven by light, went throbbing before her through a long narrow passage. Suddenly it rose higher, and the same moment Nycteris fell upon an ascending stair. She had never seen a stair before, and found going up a curious sensation. Just as she reached what seemed the top, the firefly ceased to shine, and so disappeared. She was in utter darkness once more. But when we are following the light, even its extinction is a guide. If the firefly had gone on shining, Nycteris would have seen the stair turn and would have gone up to Watho's bedroom; whereas now, feeling straight before her, she came to a latched door, which after a good deal of trying she managed to open—and stood in a maze of wondering perplexity, awe, and delight. What was it? Was it outside of her, or something taking place in her head? Before her was a very long and very narrow passage, broken up she could not tell how, and spreading out above and on all sides to an infinite height and breadth and distance—as if space itself were growing out of a trough. It was brighter than her rooms had ever been—brighter than if six alabaster lamps had been burning in them. There was a quantity of strange streaking and mottling about it, very different from the shapes on her walls. She was in a dream of pleasant perplexity, of delightful bewilderment. She could not tell whether she was upon her feet or drifting about like the firefly, driven by the pulses of an inward bliss. But she knew little as yet of her inheritance. Unconsciously, she took one step forward from the threshold, and the girl who had been from her very birth a troglodyte stood in the ravishing glory of a southern night, lit by a perfect moon—not the moon of our northern clime, but a moon like silver glowing in a furnace—a moon one could see to be a globe—not far off, a mere flat disk on the face of the blue, but hanging down halfway, and looking as if one could see all around it by a mere bending of the neck.

"It is my lamp," she said, and stood dumb

with parted lips. She looked and felt as if she had been standing there in silent ecstasy from the beginning.

"No, it is not my lamp," she said after a while; "it is the mother of all the lamps."

And with that she fell on her knees and spread out her hands to the moon. She could not in the least have told what was in her mind, but the action was in reality just a begging of the moon to be what she was—that precise incredible splendor hung in the far-off roof, that very glory essential to the being of poor girls born and bred in caverns. It was a resurrection—nay, a birth itself, to Nycteris. What the vast blue sky, studded with tiny sparks like the heads of diamond nails, could be; what the moon, looking so absolutely content with light—why, she knew less about them than you and I! but the greatest of astronomers might envy the rapture of such a first impression at the age of sixteen. Immeasurably imperfect it was, but false the impression could not be, for she saw with the eyes made for seeing, and saw indeed what many men are too wise to see.

As she knelt, something softly flapped her,

embraced her, stroked her, fondled her. She rose to her feet but saw nothing, did not know what it was. It was likest a woman's breath. For she knew nothing of the air even, had never breathed the still, newborn freshness of the world. Her breath had come to her only through long passages and spirals in the rock. Still less did she know of the air alive with motion—of that thrice-blessed thing, the wind of a summer night. It was like a spiritual wine, filling her whole being with an intoxication of purest joy. To breathe was a perfect existence. It seemed to her the light itself she drew into her lungs. Possessed by the power of the gorgeous night, she seemed at one and the same moment annihilated and glorified.

She was in the open passage or gallery that ran around the top of the garden walls, between the cleft battlements, but she did not once look down to see what lay beneath. Her soul was drawn to the vault above her with its lamp and its endless room. At last she burst into tears, and her heart was relieved, as the night itself is relieved by its lightning and rain.

And now she grew thoughtful. She must

hoard this splendor! What a little ignorance her jailers had made of her! Life was a mighty bliss, and they had scraped hers to the bare bone! They must not know that she knew. She must hide her knowledge—hide it even from her own eyes, keeping it close in her bosom, content to know that she had it, even when she could not brood on its presence, feasting her eyes with its glory. She turned from the vision, therefore, with a sigh of utter bliss, and with soft quiet steps and groping hands stole back into the darkness of the rock. What was darkness or the laziness of Time's feet to one who had seen what she had that night seen? She was lifted above all weariness—above all wrong.

When Falca entered, she uttered a cry of terror. But Nycteris called to her not to be afraid, and told her how there had come a rumbling and shaking, and the lamp had fallen. Then Falca went and told her mistress, and within an hour a new globe hung in the place of the old one. Nycteris thought it did not look so bright and clear as the former, but she made no lamentation over the change; she was far too rich to heed it. For now, prisoner as she knew herself, her heart was full of glory and gladness; at times she had to hold herself from jumping up, and going dancing and singing about the room. When she slept, instead of dull dreams, she had splendid visions. There were times, it is true, when she became restless, and impatient to look upon her riches, but then she would reason with herself, saying, "What does it matter if I sit here for ages with my poor pale lamp, when out there a lamp is burning at which ten thousand little lamps are glowing with wonder?"

She never doubted she had looked upon the day and the sun, of which she had read; and always when she read of the day and the sun, she had the night and the moon in her mind; and when she read of the night and the moon, she thought only of the cave and the lamp that hung there.

IT WAS SOME TIME BEFORE SHE HAD A SECOND opportunity of going out, for Falca since the fall of the lamp had been a little more careful, and seldom left her for long. But one night, having a little headache, Nycteris lay down upon her bed, and was lying with her eyes closed, when she heard Falca come to her, and felt she was bending over her. Disinclined to talk, she did not open her eyes, and lay quite still. Satisfied that she was asleep, Falca left her, moving so softly that her very caution made Nycteris open her eyes and look after her—just in time to see her vanish—through a picture, as it seemed, that hung on the wall a long way from the usual place of issue. She jumped up, her headache forgotten, and ran in the opposite direction; got out, groped her way to the stair, climbed, and reached the top of the wall.—Alas! the great room was not so light as the little one she had left! Why?—Sorrow of sorrows! the great lamp was gone! Had its globe fallen? and its lovely light gone out upon great wings, a resplendent firefly, oaring itself through a yet grander and lovelier room? She looked down to see if it lay anywhere broken to pieces on the carpet below; but she could not even see the carpet. But surely nothing very dreadful could have happened—no rumbling or shaking; for there were all the little lamps shining brighter than before, not one of them looking as if any unusual matter had befallen. What if each of those little lamps was growing into a big lamp, and after being a big lamp for a while, had to go out and grow a bigger lamp still—out there, beyond this *out*?—Ah! here was the living thing that could not be seen, come to her again—bigger tonight! with such loving kisses, and such liquid strokings of her cheeks and forehead, gently tossing her hair, and delicately toying with it! But it ceased, and all was still. Had it gone out? What would happen next? Perhaps the little lamps had not to grow great lamps, but to fall one by one and go out first?—With that came from below a sweet scent, then another, and another. Ah, how delicious! Perhaps they were all coming to her only on their way out after the great lamp!— Then came the music of the river, which she had been too absorbed in the sky to note the first time. What was it? Alas! alas! another sweet living thing on its way out. They were all marching slowly out in long lovely file, one after the other, each taking its leave of her as it passed! It must be so: here were more and more sweet sounds, following and fading! The whole of the *Out* was going out again; it was all going after the great lovely lamp! She would be left the only creature in the solitary day! Was there nobody to hang up a new lamp for the old one, and keep the creatures from going?—She crept back to her rock very sad. She tried to comfort herself by saying that anyhow there would be room out there; but as she said it she shuddered at the thought of *empty* room.

When next she succeeded in getting out, a half-moon hung in the east: a new lamp had come, she thought, and all would be well.

It would be endless to describe the phases of feeling through which Nycteris passed, more numerous and delicate than those of a thousand changing moons. A fresh bliss bloomed in her soul with every varying aspect of infinite nature. Ere long she began to suspect that the new moon was the old moon, gone out and come in again like herself; also that, unlike herself, it wasted and grew again; that it was indeed a live thing, subject like herself to caverns, and keepers, and solitudes, escaping and shining when it could. Was it a prison like hers it was shut in? and did it grow dark when the lamp left it? Where could be the way into it?—With that, first she began to look below, as well as above and around her; and then first noted the tops of the trees between her and the floor. There were palms with their red-fingered hands full of fruit; eucalyptus trees crowded with little boxes of powder puffs; oleanders with their half-caste roses; and orange trees with their clouds of young silver stars and

their aged balls of gold. Her eyes could see colors invisible to ours in the moonlight, and all these she could distinguish well, though at first she took them for the shapes and colors of the carpet of the great room. She longed to get down among them, now she saw they were real creatures, but she did not know how. She went along the whole length of the wall to the end that crossed the river, but found no way of going down. Above the river she stopped to gaze with awe upon the rushing water. She knew nothing of water but from what she drank and what she bathed in; and as the moon shone on the dark, swift stream, singing lustily as it flowed, she did not doubt the river was alive, a swift rushing serpent of life, going—out?— whither? And then she wondered if what was brought into her rooms had been killed that she might drink it, and have her bath in it.

Once when she stepped out upon the wall, it was into the midst of a fierce wind. The trees were all roaring. Great clouds were rushing along the skies and tumbling over the little lamps: the great lamp had not come yet. All was in tumult. The wind seized her garments and hair and shook them as if it would tear them from her. What could she have done to make the gentle creature so angry? Or was this another creature altogether—of the same kind, but hugely bigger, and of a very different temper and behavior? But the whole place was angry! Or was it that the creatures dwelling in it, the wind, and the trees, and the clouds, and the river, had all quarreled, each with all the rest? Would the whole come to confusion and disorder? But as she gazed wondering and disquieted, the moon, larger than ever she had seen her, came lifting herself above the horizon to look, broad and red, as if she, too, were swollen with anger that she had been roused from her rest by their noise, and compelled to hurry up to see what her children were about, thus rioting in her absence, lest they should rack the whole frame of things. And as she rose, the loud wind grew quieter and scolded less fiercely, the trees grew stiller and moaned with a lower complaint, and the clouds hunted and hurled themselves less wildly across the sky. And as if she were pleased that her children obeyed her very presence, the moon grew smaller as she ascended the heavenly stair; her puffed cheeks sank, her complexion grew clearer, and a sweet smile spread over her countenance, as peacefully she rose and rose. But there was treason and rebellion in her court; for ere she reached the top of her great stairs, the clouds had assembled, forgetting their late wars, and very still they were as they laid their heads together and conspired. Then combining, and lying silently in wait until she came near, they threw themselves upon her and swallowed her up. Down from the roof came spots of wet, faster and faster, and they wetted the cheeks of Nycteris; and what could they be but the tears of the moon, crying because her children were smothering her? Nycteris wept too and, not knowing what to think, stole back in dismay to her room.

The next time, she came out in fear and trembling. There was the moon still! away in the west—poor, indeed, and old, and looking dreadfully worn, as if all the wild beasts in the sky had been gnawing at her—but there she was, alive still, and able to shine!

NOWING NOTHING OF DARKNESS, OR STARS,
or moon, Photogen spent his days in hunting.
On a great white horse he swept over the grassy
plains, glorying in the sun, fighting the wind,
and killing the buffaloes.

One morning, when he happened to be on
the ground a little earlier than usual, and before
his attendants, he caught sight of an animal
unknown to him, stealing from a hollow into
which the sunrays had not yet reached. Like a
swift shadow it sped over the grass, slinking
southward to the forest. He gave chase, noted
the body of a buffalo it had half eaten, and
pursued it the harder. But with great leaps and
bounds the creature shot farther and farther

ahead of him, and vanished. Turning therefore defeated, he met Fargu, who had been following him as fast as his horse could carry him.

"What animal was that, Fargu?" he asked. "How he did run!"

Fargu answered he might be a leopard, but he rather thought from his pace and look that he was a young lion.

"What a coward he must be!" said Photogen.

"Don't be too sure of that," rejoined Fargu. "He is one of the creatures the sun makes uncomfortable. As soon as the sun is down, he will be brave enough."

He had scarcely said it, when he repented; nor did he regret it the less when he found that Photogen made no reply. But alas! said was said.

"Then," said Photogen to himself, "that contemptible beast is one of the terrors of sundown, of which Madame Watho spoke!"

He hunted all day, but not with his usual spirit. He did not ride so hard, and did not kill one buffalo. Fargu to his dismay observed also that he took every pretext for moving farther south, nearer to the forest. But all at once, the sun now sinking in the west, he seemed to change his mind, for he turned his horse's head and rode home so fast that the rest could not keep him in sight. When they arrived, they found his horse in the stable and concluded that he had gone into the castle. But he had in truth set out again by the back of it. Crossing the river a good way up the valley, he reascended to the ground they had left, and just before sunset reached the skirts of the forest.

The level orb shone straight in between the bare stems, and saying to himself he could not fail to find the beast, he rushed into the wood. But even as he entered, he turned and looked to the west. The rim of the red was touching the horizon, all jagged with broken hills. "Now," said Photogen, "we shall see"; but he said it in the face of a darkness he had not proved. The moment the sun began to sink among the spikes and saw edges, with a kind of sudden flap at his heart a fear inexplicable laid hold of the youth; and as he had never felt anything of the kind before, the very fear itself terrified him. As the sun sank, it rose like the shadow of the world and grew deeper and darker. He could not even think what it might be, so utterly did it enfeeble him. When the last flaming scimitar edge of the sun went out like a lamp, his horror seemed to blossom into very madness. Like the closing lids of an eye—for there was no twilight, and this night no moon—the terror and the darkness rushed together, and he knew them for one. He was no longer the man he had known, or rather thought himself. The courage he had had was in no sense his own—he had only had courage, not been courageous; it had left him, and he could scarcely stand—certainly not stand straight, for not one of his joints could he make stiff or keep from trembling. He was but a spark of the sun, in himself nothing.

The beast was behind him—stealing upon him! He turned. All was dark in the wood, but to his fancy the darkness here and there broke into pairs of green eyes, and he had not the power even to raise his bow hand from his side. In the strength of despair he strove to rouse courage enough—not to fight—that he did not even desire—but to run. Courage to flee home was all he could ever imagine, and it would not come. But what he had not was ignominiously given him. A cry in the wood, half a screech, half a growl, sent him running like a boar-wounded cur. It was not even himself that ran, it was the fear that had come alive in his legs; he did not know that they moved. But as he ran he grew able to run—gained courage at least to be a coward. The stars gave a little light. Over the grass he sped, and nothing followed him. "How fallen, how changed," from the youth who had climbed the hill as the sun went down! A mere contempt to himself, the self that contemned was a coward with the self it contemned! There lay the shapeless black of a buffalo, humped upon the grass. He made a wide circuit and swept on like a shadow driven in the wind. For the wind had arisen, and added to his terror: it blew from behind him. He reached the brow of the valley and shot down the steep descent like a falling star. Instantly the whole upper country behind him arose and pursued him! The wind came howling after him, filled with screams, shrieks, yells, roars, laughter, and chattering, as if all the animals of the forest were careering with it. In his ears was a trampling rush, the thunder of the hoofs of the cattle, in career from every quarter of the wide plains to the brow of the hill above him. He fled straight for the castle, scarcely with breath enough to pant.

As he reached the bottom of the valley, the moon peered up over its edge. He had never seen the moon before—except in the daytime, when he had taken her for a thin bright cloud. She was a fresh terror to him—so ghostly! so ghastly! so gruesome!—so knowing as she looked over the top of her garden wall upon the world outside! That was the night itself! the darkness alive— and after him! the horror of horrors coming down the sky to curdle his blood and turn his brain to a cinder! He gave a sob and made straight for the river, where it ran between the two walls, at the bottom of the garden. He plunged in, struggled through, clambered up the bank, and fell senseless on the grass.

ALTHOUGH NYCTERIS TOOK CARE NOT TO STAY
out long at a time, and used every precaution,
she could hardly have escaped discovery so long
had it not been that the strange attacks to which
Watho was subject had been more frequent of
late, and had at last settled into an illness which
kept her to her bed. But whether from an access
of caution or from suspicion, Falca, having now
to be much with her mistress both day and night,
took it at length into her head to fasten the door
as often as she went by her usual place of exit,
so that one night, when Nycteris pushed, she
found, to her surprise and dismay, that the wall
pushed her again, and would not let her through;
nor with all her searching could she discover

wherein lay the cause of the change. Then first she felt the pressure of her prison walls, and turning, half in despair, groped her way to the picture where she had once seen Falca disappear. There she soon found the spot by pressing upon which the wall yielded. It let her through into a sort of cellar, where was a glimmer of light from a sky whose blue was paled by the moon. From the cellar she got into a long passage, into which the moon was shining, and came to a door. She managed to open it, and to her great joy found herself in *the other place*, not on the top of the wall, however, but in the garden she had longed to enter. Noiseless as a fluffy moth she flitted away into the covert of the trees and shrubs, her bare feet welcomed by the softest of carpets, which, by the very touch, her feet knew to be alive, whence it came that it was so sweet and friendly to them. A soft little wind was out among the trees, running now here, now there, like a child that had got its will. She went dancing over the grass, looking behind her at her shadow as she went. At first she had taken it for a little black creature that made game of her, but when she perceived that it was only where she kept the moon away, and that every tree, however great and grand a creature, had also one of these strange attendants, she soon learned not to mind it, and by and by it became the source of as much amusement to her as to any kitten its tail. It was long before she was quite at home with the trees, however. At one time they seemed to disapprove of her; at another not even to know she was there, and to be altogether taken up with their own business. Suddenly, as she went from one to another of them, looking up with awe at the murmuring mystery of their branches and leaves, she spied one a little way off, which was very different from all the rest. It was white, and dark, and sparkling, and spread like a palm—a small slender palm, without much head; and it grew very fast, and sang as it grew. But it never grew any bigger, for just as fast as she could see it growing, it kept falling to pieces. When she got close to it, she discovered that it was a water tree—made of just such water as she washed with—only it was alive of course, like the river—a different sort of water from that, doubt-less, seeing the one crept swiftly along the floor, and the other shot straight up, and fell, and swallowed itself, and rose again. She put her feet into the marble basin, which was the flower-pot in which it grew. It was full of real water, living and cool—so nice, for the night was hot!

But the flowers! ah, the flowers! she was friends with them from the very first. What wonderful creatures they were!—and so kind and beautiful—always sending out such colors and such scents—red scent, and white scent, and yellow scent—for the other creatures! The one that was invisible and everywhere took such a quantity of their scents, and carried it away! yet they did not seem to mind. It was their talk, to show they were alive, and not painted like those on the walls of her rooms, and on the carpets.

She wandered along down the garden, until she reached the river. Unable then to get any further—for she was a little afraid, and justly, of the swift watery serpent—she dropped on the grassy bank, dipped her feet in the water, and felt it running and pushing against them. For a long time she sat thus, and her bliss seemed complete, as she gazed at the river and watched the broken picture of the great lamp overhead, moving up one side of the roof, to go down the other.

BEAUTIFUL MOTH BRUSHED ACROSS THE GREAT blue eyes of Nycteris. She sprang to her feet to follow it—not in the spirit of the hunter, but of the lover. Her heart—like every heart, if only its fallen sides were cleared away—was an inexhaustible fountain of love: she loved everything she saw. But as she followed the moth, she caught sight of something lying on the bank of the river, and not yet having learned to be afraid of anything, ran straight to see what it was. Reaching it, she stood amazed. Another girl like herself! But what a strange-looking girl!— so curiously dressed too!—and not able to move! Was she dead? Filled suddenly with pity, she sat down, lifted Photogen's head, laid it on her lap, and began stroking his face. Her warm hands brought him to himself. He opened his black eyes, out of which had gone all the fire, and looked up with a strange sound of fear, half moan, half gasp. But when he saw her face, he drew a deep breath and lay motionless—gazing at her: those blue marvels above him, like a better sky, seemed to side with courage and assuage his terror. At length, in a trembling, awed voice, and a half whisper, he said, "Who are you?"

"I am Nycteris," she answered.

"You are a creature of the darkness, and love the night," he said, his fear beginning to move again.

"I may be a creature of the darkness," she replied. "I hardly know what you mean. But I do not love the night. I love the day—with all my heart; and I sleep all the night long."

"How can that be?" said Photogen, rising on his elbow, but dropping his head on her lap again the moment he saw the moon; "—how can it be," he repeated, "when I see your eyes there—wide awake?"

She only smiled and stroked him, for she did not understand him, and thought he did not know what he was saying.

"Was it a dream then?" resumed Photogen, rubbing his eyes. But with that his memory came clear, and he shuddered and cried, "Oh, horrible! horrible! to be turned all at once into a coward! a shameful, contemptible, disgraceful coward! I am ashamed—ashamed—and so frightened! It is all so frightful!"

"What is so frightful?" asked Nycteris, with a smile like that of a mother to her child waked from a bad dream.

"All, all," he answered; "all this darkness and the roaring."

"My dear," said Nycteris, "there is no roaring. How sensitive you must be! What you hear is only the walking of the water, and the running about of the sweetest of all the creatures. She is invisible, and I call her Everywhere, for she goes through all the other creatures, and comforts them. Now she is amusing herself, and them too, with shaking them and kissing them, and blowing in their faces. Listen: do you call that roaring? You should hear her when she is rather angry though! I don't know why, but she is sometimes, and then she does roar a little."

"It is so horribly dark!" said Photogen, who, listening while she spoke, had satisfied himself that there was no roaring.

"Dark!" she echoed. "You should be in my room when an earthquake has killed my lamp. I do not understand. How *can* you call this dark? Let me see: yes, you have eyes, and big ones, bigger than Madame Watho's or Falca's—not so big as mine, I fancy—only I never saw mine. But then—oh, yes!—I know now what is the matter! You can't see with them, because they are so black. Darkness can't see, of course. Never mind: I will be your eyes, and teach you to see. Look here—at these lovely white things in the grass, with red sharp points all folded together into one. Oh, I love them so! I could sit looking at them all day, the darlings!"

Photogen looked close at the flowers, and thought he had seen something like them before, but could not make them out. As Nycteris had never seen an open daisy, so had he never seen a closed one.

Thus instinctively Nycteris tried to turn him away from his fear; and the beautiful creature's strange lovely talk helped not a little to make him forget it.

"You call it dark!" she said again, as if she could not get rid of the absurdity of the idea; "why, I could count every blade of the green hair—I suppose it is what the books call grass—within two yards of me! And just look at the great lamp! It is brighter than usual today, and I can't think why you should be frightened, or call it dark!"

As she spoke, she went on stroking his cheeks and hair, and trying to comfort him. But oh how miserable he was! and how plainly he looked it! He was on the point of saying that her great lamp was dreadful to him, looking like a witch, walking in the sleep of death; but he was not so ignorant as Nycteris, and knew even in the moonlight that she was a woman, though he had never seen one so young or so lovely before; and while she comforted his fear, her presence made him the more ashamed of it. Besides, not knowing her nature, he might annoy her, and make her leave him to his misery. He lay still therefore, hardly daring to move: all the little life he had seemed to come from her, and if he were to move, she might move: and if she were to leave him, he must weep like a child.

"How did you come here?" asked Nycteris, taking his face between her hands.

"Down the hill," he answered.

"Where do you sleep?" she asked.

He signed in the direction of the house. She gave a little laugh of delight.

"When you have learned not to be frightened, you will always be wanting to come out with me," she said.

She thought with herself she would ask her presently, when she had come to herself a little, how she had made her escape, for she must, of course, like herself, have got out of a cave, in which Watho and Falca had been keeping her.

"Look at the lovely colors," she went on, pointing to a rose bush, on which Photogen could not see a single flower. "They are far more beautiful—are they not?—than any of the colors upon your walls. And then they are alive, and smell so sweet!"

He wished she would not make him keep opening his eyes to look at things he could not see; and every other moment would start and grasp tight hold of her, as some fresh pang of terror shot into him.

"Come, come, dear!" said Nycteris, "you must not go on this way. You must be a brave girl, and—"

"A girl!" shouted Photogen, and started to his feet in wrath. "If you were a man, I should kill you."

"A man?" repeated Nycteris. "What is that? How could I be that? We are both girls—are we not?"

"No, I am not a girl," he answered; "—although," he added, changing his tone, and casting himself on the ground at her feet, "I have given you too good reason to call me one."

"Oh, I see!" returned Nycteris. "No, of course!—you can't be a girl: girls are not afraid—without reason. I understand now: it is because you are not a girl that you are so frightened."

Photogen twisted and writhed upon the grass.

"No, it is not," he said sulkily; "it is this horrible darkness that creeps into me, goes all through me, into the very marrow of my bones—that is what makes me behave like a girl. If only the sun would rise!"

"The sun! what is it?" cried Nycteris, now in her turn conceiving a vague fear.

Then Photogen broke into a rhapsody, in which he vainly sought to forget his.

"It is the soul, the life, the heart, the glory of the universe," he said. "The worlds dance like motes in his beams. The heart of man is strong and brave in his light, and when it departs his courage grows from him—goes with the sun, and he becomes such as you see me now."

"Then that is not the sun?" said Nycteris, thoughtfully, pointing up to the moon.

"That!" cried Photogen, with utter scorn. "I know nothing about *that*, except that it is ugly and horrible. At best it can be only the ghost of a dead sun. Yes, that is it! That is what makes it look so frightful."

"No," said Nycteris, after a long, thoughtful

pause; "you must be wrong there. I think the sun is the ghost of a dead moon, and that is how he is so much more splendid as you say.—Is there, then, another big room, where the sun lives in the roof?"

"I do not know what you mean," replied Photogen. "But you mean to be kind, I know, though you should not call a poor fellow in the dark a girl. If you will let me lie here, with my head in your lap, I should like to sleep. Will you watch me, and take care of me?"

"Yes, that I will," answered Nycteris, forgetting all her own danger.

So Photogen fell asleep.

HERE NYCTERIS SAT, AND THERE THE YOUTH
lay all night long, in the heart of the great cone-
shadow of the earth, like two pharaohs in one
pyramid. Photogen slept, and slept; and Nycteris
sat motionless lest she should wake him, and so
betray him to his fear.

The moon rode high in the blue eternity; it
was a very triumph of glorious night; the river
ran babble-murmuring in deep soft syllables;
the fountain kept rushing moonward, and blos-
soming momently to a great silvery flower,
whose petals were forever falling like snow, but
with a continuous musical clash, into the bed of
its exhaustion beneath; the wind woke, took a
run among the trees, went to sleep, and woke

again; the daisies slept on their feet at hers, but she did not know they slept; the roses might well seem awake, for their scent filled the air, but in truth they slept also, and the odor was that of their dreams; the oranges hung like gold lamps in the trees, and their silvery flowers were the souls of their yet unembodied children; the scent of the acacia blooms filled the air like the very odor of the moon herself.

At last, unused to the living air, and weary with sitting so still and so long, Nycteris grew drowsy. The air began to grow cool. It was getting near the time when she too was accustomed to sleep. She closed her eyes just a moment, and nodded—opened them suddenly wide, for she had promised to watch.

In that moment a change had come. The moon had got round and was fronting her from the west, and she saw that her face was altered, that she had grown pale, as if she too were wan with fear, and from her lofty place espied a coming terror. The light seemed to be dissolving out of her; she was dying—she was going out! And yet everything around looked strangely clear—

clearer than ever she had seen anything before; how could the lamp be shedding more light when she herself had less? Ah, that was just it! See how faint she looked! It was because the light was forsaking her, and spreading itself over the room, that she grew so thin and pale! She was giving up everything! She was melting away from the roof like a bit of sugar in water.

Nycteris was fast growing afraid, and sought refuge with the face upon her lap. How beautiful the creature was!—what to call it she could not think, for it had been angry when she called it what Watho called her. And, wonder upon wonders! now, even in the cold change that was passing upon the great room, the color as of a red rose was rising in the wan cheek. What beautiful yellow hair it was that spread over her lap! What great huge breaths the creature took! And what were those curious things it carried? She had seen them on her walls, she was sure.

Thus she talked to herself while the lamp grew paler and paler, and everything kept growing yet clearer. What could it mean? The lamp was dying—going out into the other place of which the creature in her lap had spoken, to be a sun! But why were the things growing clearer before it was yet a sun? That was the point. Was it her growing into a sun that did it? Yes! yes! it was coming death! She knew it, for it was coming upon her also! She felt it coming! What was she about to grow into? Something beautiful, like the creature in her lap? It might be! Anyhow, it must be death; for all her strength was going out of her, while all around her was growing so light she could not bear it! She must be blind soon! Would she be blind or dead first?

For the sun was rushing up behind her. Photogen woke, lifted his head from her lap, and sprang to his feet. His face was one radiant smile. His heart was full of daring—that of the hunter who will creep into the tiger's den. Nycteris gave a cry, covered her face with her hands, and pressed her eyelids close. Then blindly she stretched out her arms to Photogen, crying, "Oh, I am so frightened! What is this? It must be death! I don't wish to die yet. I love this room and the old lamp. I do not want the other place. This is terrible. I want to hide. I want to get into the sweet, soft, dark hands of all the other creatures. Ah me! ah me!"

"What is the matter with you, girl?" said Photogen, with the arrogance of all male creatures until they have been taught by the other kind. He stood looking down upon her over his bow, of which he was examining the string. "There is no fear of anything now, child! It is day. The sun is all but up. Look! he will be above the brow of yon hill in one moment more! Goodbye. Thank you for my night's lodging. I'm off. Don't be a goose. If ever I can do anything for you—and all that, you know!"

"Don't leave me; oh, don't leave me!" cried Nycteris. "I am dying! I am dying! I can't move. The light sucks all the strength out of me. And oh, I am *so* frightened!"

But already Photogen had splashed through the river, holding high his bow that it might not get wet. He rushed across the level and strained up the opposing hill. Hearing no answer, Nycteris removed her hands. Photogen had

reached the top, and the same moment the sun rays alighted upon him; the glory of the king of day crowded blazing upon the golden-haired youth. Radiant as Apollo, he stood in mighty strength, a flashing shape in the midst of flame. He fitted a glowing arrow to a gleaming bow. The arrow parted with a keen musical twang of the bowstring, and Photogen, darting after it, vanished with a shout. Up shot Apollo himself, and from his quiver scattered astonishment and exultation. But the brain of poor Nycteris was pierced through and through. She fell down in utter darkness. All around her was a flaming furnace. In despair and feebleness and agony, she crept back, feeling her way with doubt and difficulty and enforced persistence to her cell. When at last the friendly darkness of her chamber folded her about with its cooling and consoling arms, she threw herself on her bed and fell fast asleep. And there she slept on, one alive in a tomb, while Photogen, above in the sun-glory, pursued the buffaloes on the lofty plain, thinking not once of her where she lay dark and forsaken, whose presence had been his refuge, her eyes and her hands his guardians through the night. He was in his glory and his pride; and the darkness and its disgrace had vanished for a time.

UT NO SOONER HAD THE SUN REACHED THE noonstead, than Photogen began to remember the past night in the shadow of that which was at hand, and to remember it with shame. He had proved himself—and not to himself only, but to a girl as well—a coward!—one bold in the daylight, while there was nothing to fear, but trembling like any slave when the night arrived. There was, there must be, something unfair in it! A spell had been cast upon him! He had eaten, he had drunk something that did not agree with courage! In any case he had been taken unprepared! How was he to know what the going down of the sun would be like? It was no wonder he should have been surprised into terror, seeing it was what it was—in its very nature so terrible! Also, one could not see where danger might be coming from! You might be torn in pieces, carried off, or swallowed up, without even seeing where to strike a blow! Every possible excuse he caught at, eager as a self-lover to lighten his self-contempt. That day he astonished the huntsmen—terrified them with his reckless daring—all to prove to himself he was no coward. But nothing eased his shame. One thing only had hope in it—the resolve to encounter the dark in solemn earnest, now that he knew something of what it was. It was nobler to meet a recognized danger than to rush contemptuously into what seemed nothing—nobler still to encounter a nameless horror. He could conquer fear and wipe out disgrace together. For a marksman and swordsman like him, he said, one with his strength and courage, there was but danger. Defeat there was not. He knew the darkness now, and when it came he would meet it as fearless and cool as now he felt himself. And again he said, "We shall see!"

He stood under the boughs of a great beech as the sun was going down, far away over the jagged hills: before it was half down, he was trembling like one of the leaves behind him in the first sigh of the night wind. The moment the last of the glowing disk vanished, he bounded away in terror to gain the valley, and his fear grew as he ran. Down the side of the hill, an abject creature, he went bounding and rolling and running; fell rather than plunged into the river, and came to himself, as before, lying on the grassy bank in the garden.

But when he opened his eyes, there were no girl-eyes looking down into his; there were only the stars in the waste of the sunless Night—the awful all-enemy he had again dared, but could not encounter. Perhaps the girl was not yet come out of the water! He would try to sleep, for he dared not move, and perhaps when he woke he would find his head on her lap, and the beautiful dark face, with its deep blue eyes, bending over him. But when he woke he found his head on the grass, and although he sprang up with all his courage, such as it was, restored, he did not set

out for the chase with such an *élan* as the day
before; and, despite the sun-glory in his heart
and veins, his hunting was this day less eager;
he ate little, and from the first was thoughtful
even to sadness. A second time he was defeated
and disgraced! Was his courage nothing more
than the play of the sunlight on his brain? Was
he a mere ball tossed between the light and the
dark? Then what a poor contemptible creature
he was! But a third chance lay before him. If
he failed the third time, he dared not foreshadow
what he must then think of himself! It was bad
enough now—but then!

Alas! it went no better. The moment the sun
was down, he fled as if from a legion of devils.

Seven times in all, he tried to face the coming
night in the strength of the past day, and seven
times he failed—failed with such increase of
failure, with such a growing sense of ignominy,
overwhelming at length all the sunny hours and
joining night to night, that, what with misery,
self-accusation, and loss of confidence, his daylight courage too began to fade, and at length,
from exhaustion, from getting wet, and then

lying out of doors all night, and night after night—worst of all, from the consuming of the deathly fear, and the shame of shame, his sleep forsook him, and on the seventh morning, instead of going to the hunt, he crawled into the castle and went to bed. The grand health, over which the witch had taken such pains, had yielded, and in an hour or two he was moaning and crying out in delirium.

ATHO WAS HERSELF ILL, AS I HAVE SAID, AND
was the worse tempered; and besides, it is a
peculiarity of witches that what works in others
to sympathy works in them to repulsion. Also,
Watho had a poor, helpless, rudimentary spleen
of a conscience left, just enough to make her
uncomfortable, and therefore more wicked. So,
when she heard that Photogen was ill, she was
angry. Ill, indeed! after all she had done to
saturate him with the life of the system, with
the solar might itself? He was a wretched
failure, the boy! And because he was *her* failure,
she was annoyed with him, began to dislike
him, grew to hate him. She looked on him as
a painter might upon a picture, or a poet upon

a poem, which he had only succeeded in getting into an irrecoverable mess. In the hearts of witches, love and hate lie close together, and often tumble over each other. And whether it was that her failure with Photogen foiled also her plans in regard to Nycteris, or that her illness made her yet more of a devil's wife, certainly Watho now got sick of the girl too, and hated to know her about the castle.

She was not too ill, however, to go to poor Photogen's room and torment him. She told him she hated him like a serpent, and hissed like one as she said it, looking very sharp in the nose and chin, and flat in the forehead. Photogen thought she meant to kill him, and hardly ventured to take anything brought him. She ordered every ray of light to be shut out of his room; but by means of this he got a little used to the darkness. She would take one of his arrows, and now tickle him with the feather end of it, now prick him with the point till the blood ran down. What she meant finally I cannot tell, but she brought Photogen speedily to the determination of making his escape from the castle:

what he should do then he would think afterwards. Who could tell but he might find his mother somewhere beyond the forest! If it were not for the broad patches of darkness that divided day from day, he would fear nothing!

But now, as he lay helpless in the dark, ever and anon would come dawning through it the face of the lovely creature who on that first awful night nursed him so sweetly: was he never to see her again? If she was, as he had concluded, the nymph of the river, why had she not reappeared? She might have taught him not to fear the night, for plainly she had no fear of it herself! But then, when the day came, she did seem frightened—why was that, seeing there was nothing to be afraid of then? Perhaps one so much at home in the darkness was correspondingly afraid of the light! Then his selfish joy at the rising of the sun, blinding him to her condition, had made him behave to her, in ill return for her kindness, as cruelly as Watho behaved to him! How sweet and dear and lovely she was! If there were wild beasts that came out only at night, and were afraid of the light, why should there not be girls too, made the same way—who could not endure the light, as he could not bear the darkness? If only he could find her again! Ah, how differently he would behave to her! But alas! perhaps the sun had killed her—melted her—burned her up—dried her up—that was it, if she was a nymph of the river!

ROM THAT DREADFUL MORNING NYCTERIS HAD
never got to be herself again. The sudden light
had been almost death to her: and now she lay
in the dark with the memory of a terrific sharp-
ness—a something she dared scarcely recall, lest
the very thought of it should sting her beyond
endurance. But this was as nothing to the pain
which the recollection of the rudeness of the
shining creature whom she had nursed through
his fear caused her; for the moment his suffering passed over to her, and he was free, the first
use he made of his returning strength had been
to scorn her! She wondered and wondered; it
was all beyond her comprehension.

Before long, Watho was plotting evil against

her. The witch was like a sick child weary of his toy: she would pull her to pieces and see how she liked it. She would set her in the sun and see her die, like a jelly from the salt ocean cast out on a hot rock. It would be a sight to soothe her wolf-pain. One day, therefore, a little before noon, while Nycteris was in her deepest sleep, she had a darkened litter brought to the door, and in that she made two of her men carry her to the plain above. There they took her out, laid her on the grass, and left her.

Watho watched it all from the top of her high tower, through her telescope; and scarcely was Nycteris left, when she saw her sit up, and the same moment cast herself down again with her face to the ground.

"She'll have a sunstroke," said Watho, "and that'll be the end of her."

Presently, tormented by a fly, a huge-humped buffalo, with great shaggy mane, came galloping along, straight for where she lay. At the sight of the thing on the grass, he started, swerved yards aside, stopped dead, and then came slowly up, looking malicious. Nycteris lay quite still and never even saw the animal.

"Now she'll be trodden to death!" said Watho. "That's the way those creatures do." When the buffalo reached her, he sniffed at her all over and went away; then came back and sniffed again: then all at once went off as if a demon had him by the tail.

Next came a gnu, a more dangerous animal still, and did much the same; then a gaunt wild boar. But no creature hurt her, and Watho was angry with the whole creation.

At length, in the shade of her hair, the blue eyes of Nycteris began to come to themselves a little, and the first thing they saw was a comfort. I have told already how she knew the night daisies, each a sharp-pointed little cone with a red tip; and once she had parted the rays of one of them, with trembling fingers, for she was afraid she was dreadfully rude, and perhaps was hurting it; but she did want, she said to herself, to see what secret it carried so carefully hidden; and she found its golden heart. But now, right under her eyes, inside the veil of her hair, in the sweet twilight of whose blackness she could see it perfectly, stood a daisy with its red tip opened wide into a carmine ring, displaying its heart of

gold on a platter of silver. She did not at first recognize it as one of those cones come awake, but a moment's notice revealed what it was. Who then could have been so cruel to the lovely little creature as to force it open like that, and spread it heart-bare to the terrible death-lamp? Whoever it was, it must be the same that had thrown her out there to be burned to death in its fire. But she had her hair, and could hang her head, and make a small sweet night of her own about her! She tried to bend the daisy down and away from the sun, and to make its petals hang about it like her hair, but she could not. Alas! it was burned and dead already! She did not know that it could not yield to her gentle force because it was drinking life, with all the eagerness of life, from what she called the death-lamp. Oh, how the lamp burned her!

But she went on thinking—she did not know how; and by and by began to reflect that, as there was no roof to the room except that in which the great fire went rolling about, the little Red-tip must have seen the lamp a thousand times, and must know it quite well! and it had not killed it! Nay, thinking about farther, she began to ask the question whether this, in which she now saw it, might not be its more perfect condition. For not only now did the whole seem perfect, as indeed it did before, but every part showed its own individual perfection as well, which perfection made it capable of combining with the rest into the higher perfection of a whole. The flower was a lamp itself! The golden heart was the light, and the silver border was the alabaster globe, skillfully broken, and spread wide to let out the glory. Yes: the radiant shape was plainly its perfection! If, then, it was the lamp which had opened it into that shape, the lamp could not be unfriendly to it, but must be of its own kind, seeing it made it perfect! And again, when she thought of it, there was clearly no little resemblance between them. What if the flower then was the little great-grandchild of the lamp and he was loving it all the time? And what if the lamp did not mean to hurt her, only could not help it? The red tips looked as if the flower had some time or other been hurt: what if the lamp was making the best it could of her—

opening her out somehow like the flower? She would bear it patiently, and see. But how coarse the color of the grass was! Perhaps, however, her eyes not being made for the bright lamp, she did not see them as they were! Then she remembered how different were the eyes of the creature that was not a girl and was afraid of the darkness! Ah, if the darkness would only come again, all arms, friendly and soft everywhere about her! She would wait and wait, and bear, and be patient.

She lay so still that Watho did not doubt she had fainted. She was pretty sure she would be dead before the night came to revive her.

IXING HER TELESCOPE ON THE MOTIONLESS
form, that she might see it at once when the
morning came, Watho went down from the
tower to Photogen's room. He was much better
by this time, and before she left him, he had
resolved to leave the castle that very night. The
darkness was terrible indeed, but Watho was
worse than even the darkness, and he could not
escape in the day. As soon, therefore, as the
house seemed still, he tightened his belt, hung
to it his hunting knife, put a flask of wine and
some bread in his pocket, and took his bow and
arrows. He got from the house and made his
way at once up to the plain. But what with his
illness, the terrors of the night, and his dread

of the wild beasts, when he got to the level he could not walk a step further, and sat down, thinking it better to die than to live. In spite of his fears, however, sleep contrived to overcome him, and he fell at full length on the soft grass.

He had not slept long when he woke with such a strange sense of comfort and security that he thought the dawn at last must have arrived. But it was dark night about him. And the sky—no, it was not the sky, but the blue eyes of his naiad looking down upon him! Once more he lay with his head in her lap, and all was well, for plainly the girl feared the darkness as little as he the day.

"Thank you," he said. "You are like live armor to my heart; you keep the fear off me. I have been very ill since then. Did you come up out of the river when you saw me cross?"

"I don't live in the water," she answered. "I live under the pale lamp, and I die under the bright one."

"Ah, yes! I understand now," he returned. "I would not have behaved as I did last time if I had understood; but I thought you were mocking me; and I am so made that I cannot help being frightened at the darkness. I beg your pardon for leaving you as I did, for, as I say, I did not understand. Now I believe you were really frightened. Were you not?"

"I was, indeed," answered Nycteris, "and shall be again. But why you should be, I cannot in the least understand. You must know how gentle and sweet the darkness is, how kind and friendly, how soft and velvety! It holds you to its bosom and loves you. A little while ago, I lay faint and dying under your hot lamp.—What is it you call it?"

"The sun," murmured Photogen. "How I wish he would make haste!"

"Ah! do not wish that. Do not, for my sake, hurry him. I can take care of you from the darkness, but I have no one to take care of me from the light.—As I was telling you, I lay dying in the sun. All at once I drew a deep breath. A cool wind came and ran over my face. I looked up. The torture was gone, for the death-lamp itself was gone. I hope he does not die and grow brighter yet. My terrible headache was all gone, and my sight was come back. I felt as if I were new made. But I did not get up at once, for I was tired still. The grass grew cool about me and turned soft in color. Something wet came upon it, and it was now so pleasant to my feet that I rose and ran about. And when I had been running about a long time, all at once I found you lying, just as I had been lying a little while before. So I sat down beside you to take care of you, till your life—and my death—should come again."

"How good you are, you beautiful creature!— Why, you forgave me before ever I asked you!" cried Photogen.

Thus they fell a-talking, and he told her what he knew of his history, and she told him what she knew of hers, and they agreed they must get away from Watho as far as ever they could.

"And we must set out at once," said Nycteris.

"The moment the morning comes," returned Photogen.

"We must not wait for the morning," said Nycteris, "for then I shall not be able to move, and what would you do the next night? Besides, Watho sees best in the daytime. Indeed, you must come now, Photogen.—You must."

"I cannot; I dare not," said Photogen. "I cannot move. If I but lift my head from your lap, the very sickness of terror seizes me."

"I shall be with you," said Nycteris, soothingly. "I will take care of you till your dreadful sun comes, and then you may leave me, and go away as fast as you can. Only please put me in a dark place first, if there is one to be found."

"I will never leave you again, Nycteris," cried Photogen. "Only wait till the sun comes, and brings me back my strength, and we will go together, and never, never part anymore."

"No, no," persisted Nycteris; "we must go now. And you must learn to be strong in the dark as well as in the day, else you will always be only half brave. I have begun already—not to fight your sun, but to try to get at peace with him, and understand what he really is, and what he means with me—whether to hurt me or to make the best of me. You must do the same with my darkness."

"But you don't know what mad animals there are away there towards the south," said Photogen. "They have huge green eyes, and they would eat you up like a bit of celery, you beautiful creature!"

"Come, come! you must," said Nycteris, "or I shall have to pretend to leave you, to make you come. I have seen the green eyes you speak of, and I will take care of you from them."

"You! How can you do that? If it were day now, I could take care of you from the worst of them. But as it is, I can't even see them for this abominable darkness. I could not see your lovely eyes but for the light that is in them; that lets me see straight into heaven through them. They are windows into the very heaven beyond the sky. I believe they are the very place where the stars are made."

"You come then, or I shall shut them," said Nycteris, "and you shan't see them anymore till you are good. Come. If you can't see the wild beasts, I can."

"You can! and you ask me to come!" cried Photogen.

"Yes," answered Nycteris. "And more than that, I see them long before they can see me, so that I am able to take care of you."

"But how?" persisted Photogen. "You can't shoot with bow and arrow, or stab with a hunting knife."

"No, but I can keep out of the way of them all. Why, just when I found you, I was having a game with two or three of them at once. I see, and scent them too, long before they are near me—long before they can see or scent me."

"You don't see or scent any now, do you?" said Photogen uneasily, rising on his elbow.

"No—none at present. I will look," replied Nycteris, and sprang to her feet.

"Oh, oh! do not leave me—not for a moment," cried Photogen, straining his eyes to keep her face in sight through the darkness.

"Be quiet, or they will hear you," she returned. "The wind is from the south, and they cannot scent us. I have found out all about that. Ever since the dear dark came, I have been amusing myself with them, getting every now and then just into the edge of the wind, and letting one have a sniff of me."

"Oh, horrible!" cried Photogen. "I hope you will not insist on doing so anymore. What was the consequence?"

"Always, the very instant, he turned with flashing eyes, and bounded towards me—only he could not see me, you must remember. But my eyes being so much better than his, I could see him perfectly well, and would run away around him until I scented him, and then I knew he could not find me anyhow. If the wind were to turn, and run the other way now, there might be a whole army of them down upon us, leaving no room to keep out of their way. You had better come."

She took him by the hand. He yielded and rose, and she led him away. But his steps were feeble, and as the night went on, he seemed more and more ready to sink.

"Oh dear! I am so tired! and so frightened!" he would say.

"Lean on me," Nycteris would return, putting her arm around him, or patting his cheek. "Take a few steps more. Every step away from the castle is clear gain. Lean harder on me. I am quite strong and well now."

So they went on. The piercing night-eyes of Nycteris descried not a few pairs of green ones gleaming like holes in the darkness, and many a round she made to keep far out of their way; but she never said to Photogen she saw them. Carefully she kept him off the uneven places, and on the softest and smoothest of the grass, talking to him gently all the way as they went—of the lovely flowers and the stars—how comfortable the flowers looked, down in their green beds, and how happy the stars up in their blue beds!

When the morning began to come, he began to grow better, but was dreadfully tired with walking instead of sleeping, especially after being so long ill. Nycteris too, what with supporting him, what with growing fear of the light which was beginning to ooze out of the east, was very tired. At length, both equally exhausted, neither was able to help the other. As if by consent they stopped. Embracing each the other, they stood in the midst of the wide grassy land, neither of them able to move a step, each supported only by the leaning weakness of the other, each ready to fall if the other should move. But while the one grew weaker still, the other had begun to grow stronger. When the tide of the night began to ebb, the tide of the day began to flow; and now the sun was rushing to the horizon, borne upon its foaming billows. And ever as he came, Photogen revived. At last the sun shot up into the air, like a bird from the hand of the Father of Lights. Nycteris gave a cry of pain and hid her face in her hands.

"Oh me!" she sighed; "I am *so* frightened! The terrible light stings so!"

But the same instant, through her blindness, she heard Photogen give a low exultant laugh, and the next felt herself caught up; she who all night long had tended and protected him like a child was now in his arms, borne along like a baby, with her head lying on his shoulder. But she was the greater, for suffering more, she feared nothing.

A T THE VERY MOMENT WHEN PHOTOGEN CAUGHT up Nycteris, the telescope of Watho was angrily sweeping the tableland. She swung it from her in rage and, running to her room, shut herself up. There she anointed herself from top to toe with a certain ointment; shook down her long red hair, and tied it around her waist; then began to dance, whirling around and around faster and faster, growing angrier and angrier, until she was foaming at the mouth with fury. When Falca went looking for her, she could not find her anywhere.

As the sun rose, the wind slowly changed and went around, until it blew straight from the north. Photogen and Nycteris were drawing near

the edge of the forest, Photogen still carrying Nycteris, when she moved a little on his shoulder uneasily and murmured in his ear.

"I smell a wild beast—that way, the way the wind is coming."

Photogen turned, looked back towards the castle, and saw a dark speck on the plain. As he looked, it grew larger: it was coming across the grass with the speed of the wind. It came nearer and nearer. It looked long and low, but that might be because it was running at a great stretch. He set Nycteris down under a tree, in the black shadow of its bole, strung his bow, and picked out his heaviest, longest, sharpest arrow. Just as he set the notch on the string, he saw that the creature was a tremendous wolf, rushing straight at him. He loosened his knife in its sheath, drew another arrow halfway from the quiver, lest the first should fail, and took his aim—at a good distance, to leave time for a second chance. He shot. The arrow rose, flew straight, descended, struck the beast, and started again into the air, doubled like a letter V. Quickly Photogen snatched the other, shot, cast his bow from him, and drew his knife. But the arrow was in the brute's chest, up to the feather; it tumbled heels over head with a great thud of its back on the earth, gave a groan, made a struggle or two, and lay stretched out motionless.

"I've killed it, Nycteris," cried Photogen. "It is a great red wolf."

"Oh, thank you!" answered Nycteris feebly from behind the tree. "I was sure you would. I was not a bit afraid."

Photogen went up to the wolf. It *was* a monster! But he was vexed that his first arrow had behaved so badly, and was the less willing to lose the one that had done him such good service: with a long and a strong pull, he drew it from the brute's chest. Could he believe his eyes? There lay—no wolf, but Watho, with her hair tied around her waist! The foolish witch had made herself invulnerable, as she supposed, but had forgotten that, to torment Photogen therewith, she had handled one of his arrows. He ran back to Nycteris and told her.

She shuddered and wept, and would not look.

THERE WAS NOW NO OCCASION TO FLY A STEP farther. Neither of them feared anyone but Watho. They left her there and went back. A great cloud came over the sun, and rain began to fall heavily, and Nycteris was much refreshed, grew able to see a little, and with Photogen's help walked gently over the cool wet grass.

They had not gone far before they met Fargu and the other huntsmen. Photogen told them he had killed a great red wolf, and it was Madame Watho. The huntsmen looked grave, but gladness shone through.

"Then," said Fargu, "I will go and bury my mistress."

But when they reached the place, they found she was already buried—in the maws of sundry birds and beasts which had made their breakfast of her.

Then Fargu, overtaking them, would, very wisely, have Photogen go to the king and tell him the whole story. But Photogen, yet wiser than Fargu, would not set out until he had married Nycteris; "for then," he said, "the king himself can't part us; and if ever two people couldn't do the one without the other, those two are Nycteris and I. She has got to teach me to be a brave man in the dark, and I have got to look after her until she can bear the heat of the sun, and he helps her to see, instead of blinding her."

They were married that very day. And the next day they went together to the king and told him the whole story. But whom should they find at the court but the father and mother of Photogen, both in high favor with the king and queen. Aurora nearly died with joy, and told them all how Watho had lied and made her believe her child was dead.

No one knew anything of the father or mother

of Nycteris; but when Aurora saw in the lovely girl her own azure eyes shining through night and its clouds, it made her think strange things, and wonder how even the wicked themselves may be a link to join together the good. Through Watho, the mothers, who had never seen each other, had changed eyes in their children.

The king gave them the castle and lands of Watho, and there they lived and taught each other for many years that were not long. But hardly had one of them passed, before Nycteris had come to love the day best, because it was the clothing and crown of Photogen, and she saw that the day was greater than the night, and the sun more lordly than the moon; and Photogen had come to love the night best, because it was the mother and home of Nycteris.

"But who knows," Nycteris would say to Photogen, "that when we go out, we shall not go into a day as much greater than your day as your day is greater than my night?"